UNICORN TALES
Callie's Magical Flight

Callie trotted over to a trough. She took a drink, lapping up the warm, glittering pink cocoa made from the special holly berries that only grew in the cold, snowy climate of Wintersend. "If only I could fly," she said. "Then I could be like the other pegacorns."

The Unicorn Tales series

UNICORN TALES
Callie's Magical Flight

AMIE BORST
illustrated by Roch Hercka

Copyright © 2019 by Amie Borst
Illustration © 2019 by Roch Hercka
Cover typography: We Got You Covered Book Designs

All rights reserved. No part of this publication may be
reproduced, distributed, or transmitted in any form
without the prior written permission of the author.

This book is a work of fiction. Names, characters, places,
and incidents are either products of the author's
imagination or are used fictitiously. Any resemblance to
actual events, locales or persons, living or dead, is entirely
coincidental.

Summary: When a shift in seasons threatens the Kingdom
of Wintersend, Callie, a peg acorn afraid of flying, must
choose between playing it safe or saving her kingdom.
BISAC: JUVENILE FICTION/Animals/Mythical.
JUVENILE FICTION/Legends, Myths &
Fables/General. JUVENILE FICTION/Social
Themes/Self Esteem.
For more information about this title, write us at Mystery
Goose Press P.O. Box 86627 Vint Hill, VA 20187

Printed in the United States of America.
Library of Congress Control Number: 2019940947
Paperback ISBN: 978-1-948882-07-1
Also available as an ebook.

CALLIE'S MAGICAL FLIGHT

AMIE BORST

Illustrated by
ROCH HERCKA

Isle of Avomea

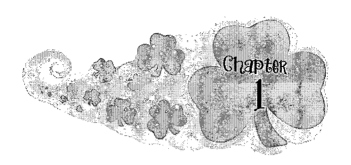

Chapter 1

The Kingdom of Wintersend in the Isle of Avonlea was a magical wonderland. Silvery clouds blanketed the sky. Mount Wintersend, the highest of the snow-capped mountains, stood straight and tall in the distance. Dreamsicle Pond invited all to skate and play. Perfectly shaped snowflakes danced in the air. Juicy pink hollyberries grew on blue-green holly trees. It was a winter delight. There was no better place for a pega-corn to live than in the Kingdom of Wintersend.

Callie whinnied with joy as she watched the snowflakes race to the ground. Some flakes were star-shaped while others were more like flowers. All were beautiful to Callie. She sighed heavily. Her warm breath came out like a puff of smoke in the cold air. It was the perfect day to make a snow fairy. Callie rolled in the snow, creating a figure with large wings.

"Come fly with me," Maribel said as she pranced toward Callie, shaking her golden mane. Maribel was one of Callie's friends and they often went skating on Dreamsicle pond together.

Startled, Callie sprung to her feet.

Maribel circled Callie's head, stirring powdery snow into the air. Some of Maribel's other friends giggled as they darted about in the air. "What are you waiting for?"

Callie shook the snow from her white fur, sending a flurry of flakes into the air. Maribel had never asked her to go flying before. Her friend couldn't have known that Callie hadn't tried to fly yet. "Not today, Maribel."

"Are you afraid?" Maribel asked.

Yes, Callie thought. *I am afraid*. All of her pegacorn friends in the Kingdom of Wintersend could fly. They hadn't been afraid. She longed to soar through the clouds like the other winged unicorns, but she had too many questions. What if her wings weren't strong enough and she fell? What if she went too high and couldn't come back down? Would she be able to control her own wings? Callie didn't answer her friend. She didn't want to admit she was afraid but she didn't want to lie, either.

It was almost as if Maribel could hear Callie's thoughts because she said, "You shouldn't be afraid to fly."

Callie lowered her head.

"We're flying to the top of Mount Wintersend to see King Hollyberry," said Maribel.

Callie looked at her friend and shook her head. "Go on without me. I'll stay here and munch on hollyberries and colorful clover."

"The hollyberries and clover can wait," Maribel said. "Rumor has it that winter is going to end. We want to find out if it's true."

"No more winter?" Callie had never heard this before. Surely, it couldn't be true. If winter vanished, then there'd be no more ice-skating on the pond, no more snow on the ground, and no more magical hollyberries to feed them. What would come of the other kingdoms? The unicorns in Springsmorn needed winter's frost to keep away the weeds in the sparkle fruit orchard. Winter's passing clouds gave The Kingdom of Summerstart much needed rain to help the colorful clover grow. Even the Kingdom of Autumnseve benefitted from winter's chill in the purple pumpkin patch. "That can't be possible. Avonlea would be in great danger."

"Well, there's only one way to find out. We must ask King Hollyberry." Maribel lifted higher into the sky. "If you change your mind, we're meeting at the Crystal Barn."

"I'll wait for your return," Callie said. "Bring me the news from the king, please."

"Of course," said Maribel. She turned in the air and flew toward the mountain range. Her friends followed close behind.

Callie trotted over to a trough. She took a drink, lapping up the warm, glittering pink cocoa made from the special hollyberries that only grew in the cold, snowy climate of Wintersend. "If only I could fly," she said. "Then I could be like the other pegacorns. I could go with them and learn the truth about winter from King Hollyberry."

As Callie thought about this, a light breeze

blew and it carried a snowflake, which landed on her nose. It tickled and Callie laughed. The snowflake quickly melted away. She watched as gray clouds lifted, parting to reveal a blue sky. There were no more snowflakes anywhere in sight!

She reared up on her hind legs and stretched her wings. *Could it be true? Was winter really ending?* Callie wondered.

As she flapped her wings, the air around her stirred into giant waves. A few young sprouts of grass peeked out from the snow and bowed in response. Callie nodded in return. A gust of wind blew straight at Callie and she struggled to gain her footing. Her wings beat fast, and her front hooves began to lift off the ground. Callie's heart fluttered. She wasn't ready yet. She struggled against the wind but brought her hooves safely down.

"That was a close one," Callie said, pawing the earth with her shimmering hoof. Sparks of glitter shot out. Callie blinked and looked down. A beautiful ice flower, with two large petals and a stamen in the center, appeared. "Whoa," she whinnied. She pawed at the ground again but nothing happened. "That was odd."

"What's odd?" chirped Callie's friend, Noelle, a lovely red bird with an unruly crest on top of her head. Noelle's beak had a black stripe, which made her look like she was always smiling. Her cheeks were blushed a sweet shade of pink.

"Hello, Noelle," Callie said as she shook her lavender-colored mane. "The grass." She pointed at the spot where her hoof had just been. The patch glistened with the fresh ice flower. It looked so out of place compared to the rest of the grass, which was coated in a light dusting of snow. "There's an ice flower there."

"An ice flower? Well, that certainly is strange," Noelle said. She darted onto the branch of another tree and ruffled her wing feathers. "Sounds like a mystery we need to solve."

Chapter 2

"Good idea," Callie said. Flying could wait. The mystery of the ice flower was much more important. Plus, it was a good excuse to avoid facing her fear.

"Let's think first. Maybe if we come up with some questions, we'll find we have some answers." Noelle chirped as she tidied her nest. She darted to the ground and returned with a beak full of straw. After carefully placing it in her nest, she said, "What do you think caused it?"

Callie wasn't sure why it happened. "The wind almost blew me into the air but I brought myself safely back down. When I landed, there was an ice flower beneath my hoof."

"Beneath your hoof?" Noelle chirped so

loud, she surprised herself. She hid her beak with her wing and laughed.

Callie laughed, too.

"Hmmm…well, back to the flower." Noelle paced back and forth on the branch, tapping a feathered wing to her head. "It's getting colder. Maybe that's it."

"Maribel said winter is ending. It's even stopped snowing." Callie shivered in the breeze. "The air is colder though. Perhaps you're right."

"An end to winter?" Noelle stopped in her tracks and froze. She looked up at the blue sky. "Hmmm….it does appear as if winter is ending. What if it's something else?"

Callie trotted over to a trough filled with colorful clovers of various sizes and colors. "What do you think it could be?"

"I'm not sure," Noelle said. "But we're going to find out."

Callie swished her tail as she munched on the clover. "How are we going to do that?" Her mouth was full and some of the clovers poked out between her lips.

"Maybe we should start by going to

Dreamsicle Pond," Noelle flew onto Callie's back. "We can see if the ice is the same."

"That's a good idea." Callie nudged the ice flower. "Maybe we should bring this with us. Then we can compare them."

Noelle nodded in agreement. She darted to the ground and pecked the ice flower free. Then she carried it in her beak and flew to Callie's head. She placed the ice flower carefully in Callie's mane. Noelle hopped up to Callie's crystal horn and perched there for the journey. "I'm ready," she said.

Callie walked off down the glittering cobblestone path. Her hooves clicked with each step making a steady four beat rhythm. Noelle tweeted along. Soon they began to sing together the motto of the land.

Kingdom of Wintersend, how we love thee.
Kingdom of Wintersend, oh how lovely.
Friends are kind and friends are winsome.
Always in the Wintersend Kingdom.

*T*hey rounded a corner and continued past a giant evergreen tree. A coating of snow glistened on its branches. The comforting fragrance of juniper tickled Callie's nose and she came to a screeching halt as she sneezed. "It always does that." She laughed with a loud neigh and flicked her tail.

"We're almost there," Noelle said. She tweeted and chirped with glee. "Soon we'll be able to compare the ice. Then maybe we can solve the mystery."

"Agreed." Callie started down the path again. In her excitement, her trot changed to a canter.

As the pond came into view, Callie pointed. "There it is!" A gust of wind suddenly collided into them. It sent Noelle sailing and she flapped her feathered wings, as she bounced about in the air.

"Hold on," Callie called as she trotted up to her. "I'll catch you."

Noelle landed safely on Callie's horn. "Thank you, friend," she said with a tweet.

They continued on the path and just as the two were about to reach the lake, another blast of wind smacked into Callie. She reared up on her hind legs and the ice flower fell from her mane. It crashed to the ground and shattered into tiny pieces. "The flower!" Callie cried. The wind blew harder and she flapped her wings as she tried to steady herself.

"Don't worry about the flower. Just brace against the wind," Noelle chirped as the wind blew her, too. She hovered in the air as she held onto Callie's mane. "Steady," she called. "Steady, Callie."

"I can't," Callie neighed.

"If you lean into it, the wind will help you take flight." Noelle let go of Callie's mane and floated in the breeze. "Like this," she said. Noelle looked comfortable and at ease with her wings, unlike Callie who fought against them. "Now you try."

"Nooo!" Callie neighed again. Her wings flapped uncontrollably, nearly lifting her off the ground. Even though she'd wanted to try, Callie wasn't quite prepared. "I'm not ready," she cried. The wind stopped suddenly, and

Callie safely lowered herself. As soon as her hooves touched the earth, glittery sparks shot out.

"Whoa." Noelle gave a long whistle as she stared wide-eyed at the sparkles Callie had created. "I saw that."

Oh no! Callie thought. *My friend knows my secret. She knows I'm afraid to fly.* "What did you see?" Callie felt embarrassed and hung her head. When she glanced down, she saw something shiny beneath her hoof.

"Look! It's another ice flower," Noelle cried. "And it came from you!"

Chapter 3

"The flower came from me?" Callie lifted her hoof and looked at the flower, puzzled. "Why...I mean...how do you think that happened?"

"I'm not sure," Noelle said as she paused, tapping her feathered-wing to her forehead. "But I think it might mean something very special."

"Special?" Callie perked up. "What kind of special?"

"We're going to find out," Noelle said. "Try it again."

Callie pawed at the ground, but nothing happened. "I don't know how."

"Maybe if you jump up?"

That idea scared Callie. If she jumped, the wind could catch her wings. Then she might have to fly. She knew she needed to try, but she was still too afraid. "I don't think jumping will work."

"You won't know until you try." Noelle looked Callie in her eyes. "When I was a fledgling, I was afraid to learn how to fly. Mother bird gave me lots of encouragement. Then I wasn't so scared. Once I finally took flight, I was glad I did. What's a bird if not for its wings?"

That was a good question, Callie thought. Certainly, the same was true of pegacorns. For Callie knew flight was what made the other pegacorns so special. "What's a pegacorn if not for its wings?" Callie whispered.

"Exactly!" Noelle tweeted. "Jumping can't be so hard, now can it? Come on now. Give it a try."

"It doesn't have to be a big jump, does it?" Callie turned her head, glancing at her friend. "Just a small one?"

"A small one will do fine."

Callie sighed with relief. A small jump meant she didn't have to go so high. Then she wouldn't be at risk of flying. The wind had calmed so Callie knew she wouldn't need to use her wings to fight against it. That had been risky in the past. She reared up on her hind legs and quickly leapt into the air.

"That's it!" Noelle tweeted. "Now land!"

Callie brought her front hooves down to the ground.

Nothing happened.

No sparkles.

No ice flower.

Nothing.

"It didn't work," Callie said.

"A small jump wasn't enough. You should jump higher. Can you leap across that broken fence over there?" Noelle pointed to a wooden railing that circled around the pond.

"I can try." Callie trotted toward it as Noelle perched in a hollyberry tree. Callie inspected the fence, backed up a few steps, then galloped straight at it. She glided across the railing, landing on all four hooves. She glanced down at the ground, but there weren't any ice flowers in the grass. "That didn't work either."

Noelle put the tip of her wing in the air.

"There's no breeze," she said, matter-of-factly. "Perhaps that's the difference."

Callie was afraid to admit that Noelle was right. If she did, she might have to fly. She wasn't ready for that. "No," she said as she shook her head. "I don't think it's that."

"Well, we won't know until another breeze comes our way," Noelle said as she flew from branch to fence post. "In the meantime, let's get that ice." She darted off toward Dreamsicle Pond and Callie trotted to keep up with her.

When they reached the pond, the two stood at the water's edge. It was frozen solid.

"We could throw rocks at the pond to chip a piece of the ice free." Noelle picked up a pebble with her beak. She dropped it onto the pond. It made a soft tinkling sound.

"I don't think that's going to work," Callie said. She pawed at a large rock sitting nearby. "Maybe we can roll this one."

Noelle flew to the ground next to the boulder and tried to push it with her wing. Callie nudged it with her nose. The rock didn't budge.

"That's not going to work, either," Noelle said, sitting on top of the rock.

"You're probably right." Callie chuffed as she shook her mane. She pranced in place, lifting her hooves and lowering them. Each step flattened the grass.

"I have an idea!" Noelle said as she watched Callie's hooves leave marks in the field. "What if you tried stomping on the pond?"

"I can do that!" Callie walked to the edge of the pond and lifted her front leg.

"Be careful! You don't want to fall in."

Callie nodded. She brought her foot down hard and a small spot of ice shattered in one, quick move. "That was easy!"

Noelle picked up the piece of ice and carried it in her beak. Then she tucked it safely into Callie's mane. "Hurry, before it melts!"

allie trotted back down the path to the ice flower she had created. "Has it melted?"

Noelle dropped the piece of ice on the ground. "Not yet."

"Good." Callie nudged the ice with her hoof so it was right next to the ice flower. "Let's compare."

Noelle was much smaller than Callie so she could get a closer look. She hopped over to one and tapped her wing to her beak. "Hmmmmm." She hopped to the other and wiped her wing across her head. "Very interesting." She hopped between them and turned her head side to side. "They're very different." Noelle then flew up and circled Callie as she whispered, "See the way the ice flower glitters and sparkles?"

"It does!" Callie whinnied with excitement.

"Shhhh. Not so loud." Noelle rubbed her ear.

"The ice from the pond is dull and milky," Callie said, making note of the difference.

"Exactly. There's something very special about that ice flower," Noelle said.

"I think so, too." Callie squinted as she inspected the two pieces of ice.

"I have an idea!"

"You do?"

Noelle nodded and flapped her wings. "We should go to the top of Mount Wintersend and ask King Hollyberry."

"Oh no," Callie gasped. Going to see the king would mean she'd finally have to learn to fly. The only other way was a dangerous path.

"What's wrong?" Noelle studied her friend.

"Asking the king for help is a very important mission. He doesn't have time for silly questions. He especially doesn't have time for nonsense." *We must make sure this is important enough to trouble the king,* Callie thought. Plus,

Maribel and her friends were on their way there to ask about the end of winter. Maybe the king would be annoyed with so many visitors. "Do you really think it's a good idea?"

"Of course it is! The king knows everything!" Noelle bounced with excitement.

I hope the path isn't too dangerous, Callie thought. If the wind caught her wings, she might have to fly. The mountain was terribly high. What if she fell? Still, she really wanted answers to this magical ice flower. The king was the only one who could help. "Maybe we should bring the king a gift."

"That's a good idea," Noelle said. "What should we bring?"

Callie thought long and hard. King Hollyberry had everything. The gift had to be very special. Something he'd never seen before. "I know! Maybe we could give him the ice flower."

"Excellent!" Noelle chirped. "I'll peck it free from the grass and then we can be on our way."

This day had certainly held many surprises. The threat of winter's end. The clear, blue skies. The ice flower. Callie felt nervous about adding a journey to see the king to her very unusual day. From what she'd heard, it was a difficult journey, up a very steep and treacherous mountain path. "What if King Hollyberry is angry?"

"Why would he be angry?" Noelle asked with a chirp.

"Maybe he won't think the flower is special. He'll be angry that we've wasted his time."

Noelle carried the flower in her beak and flew up to Callie's head. She placed the flower in Callie's mane where it was safe and snug. "Of course it's special! But we'll have to go quickly so it doesn't melt."

"I will go as fast as I can," Callie said as she stepped backward. She reared up on her hind legs with a loud whinny. She brought her legs back down and as soon as her front hooves touched the earth, she galloped off.

The wind blew into Noelle and she steadied herself on top of Callie's head. "That's it, Callie! At this speed, we'll be there in no time!" she tweeted.

"Then we can show the king the ice

flower!" Callie was overjoyed. They would soon have answers! She galloped faster. She raced past the pond, over the fence, through the village, and around the park until they reached the base of the mountain.

"You sure are fast," Noelle chirped. "I've never known a pegacorn to gallop as fast as you."

Callie blushed. "I didn't know I could be that fast."

"Well you are," Noelle said. "Now let's go see the king."

*C*allie stared up at Mount Wintersend, the tallest in the kingdom, even the tallest on the entire island of Avonlea. The mountains in the Kingdom of Summerstart were beautiful, rolling green hills. They were short and wide, unlike Mount Wintersend which was marked with sharp snow-covered peaks.

"I'm not sure I can do it," Callie said as she studied the jagged cliffs. "That's a long way up."

"It is quite high," Noelle said as she flew from Callie's horn to a tree branch. She collected some straw and began to weave it together.

"What are you doing?" Callie asked.

Noelle weaved a piece of straw here, another piece there. "I'm making a bag."

"Why would you need to do that?"

"Just wait." Noelle held up the little straw bag. "For the ice flower. It'll keep it safe." She tucked the flower inside and then looped one end of the bag over Callie's horn and buried it safely in her mane.

"Excellent idea!" Callie watched her friend shake the excess straw from her feathers. "Now, let's be on our way." Noelle began to tweet the motto of Wintersend again.

Callie froze in place and stared up at the mountain. "I don't know if I can do it," she said.

"You *can* do it. I'll help you." Noelle chirped. "Stay close to the mountain and don't stray from the path. Just think, soon you'll have answers to your questions."

Callie nodded. The thought of climbing to such heights scared her more than she wanted to admit, but she so desperately wanted an answer from the king. If he had knowledge of the ice flower then maybe he'd even be able to help her fly. *If I could only learn to face my fears,* she thought, *maybe I could do anything.*

"Let's go," Callie said, chomping her teeth together. She dug her hooves in and started the dangerous climb up the mountain with Noelle perched atop her horn.

They rounded the first turn and wind whipped at them. Callie's face stung with the bitter cold. Still, she pressed forward. The ground was covered in knee-deep snow. Icicles hung from the cliffs overhead. Wind blew and blew, bringing with it hard little pellets of hail. Callie kept her head down to protect her eyes. She took another step and shivered. "I'm cold."

"Me, too," Noelle said, her voice so tiny and faint in the wind.

"Climb down from my horn," Callie said. "If you nestle into my mane, my fur will keep you warm."

"Thank you, Callie." Noelle inched her way down Callie's horn, holding on tight as the wind blew. She reached Callie's mane and snuggled in. "I'm much warmer now," she said, holding on for safety as Callie continued to climb the mountain.

"You're welcome, friend." Although Callie was still cold, she was glad Noelle was safe and warm. She kept her head down as she rounded another corner. "Maybe Maribel was wrong. It doesn't seem like winter is ending. It's much too cold and snowy."

"It's always colder on the mountain," Noelle said. "Even if Maribel is right and winter were to end, we wouldn't feel it on the mountain."

"I almost wish Maribel were right." Callie's face burned from each slap of the wind.

"Never fear!" Noelle said with a tweet. "I see a light ahead! Just a little further."

Callie thought of the warmth the light would bring, and it renewed her energy. She began to trot, but the mountain path was icy and she slipped. As soon as she regained her footing, she took each step more carefully.

"Is that King Hollyberry's light?" Callie asked.

"I don't think so," Noelle said. "The king

lives at the very top of Mount Wintersend. We're only part way there."

"Then who do you think the light belongs to?" Callie asked.

"It's mine," a voice said. It seemed to be carried on the wind as there was no one in sight.

Callie stumbled back, shivering in fear. "Who are you?"

"I am the good fairy of Wintersend."

"Fairy?" Noelle popped up.

"Yes," the voice whispered.

"Be careful, Callie," Noelle whispered. "Fairies are known to be cunning."

"Don't be silly, little bird." The voice laughed. "Only sprites are cunning. Fairies are fair and kind."

"She's being cunning," Noelle warned. "Don't trust her."

The voice laughed again. "Would someone who's cunning grant you three wishes?"

"Three wishes?" Callie reared up with excitement. "I would wish for warmth."

"Be careful," Noelle said. "I wouldn't trust her."

"Still?" The fairy's voice grew louder until she was standing in front of them. She wore a shimmering white gown that sparkled like freshly fallen snow. Snowflakes trimmed the hem of her gown like lace. The fairy held an icicle wand in her hand and waved it overhead. "My name is Fairy Princess Snowflurry. I saw your struggle on the mountain path. I've come to help you. Now, let's warm you up a bit." She shook her wand again and made a gift from the snow. Two mugs of sparkling pink cocoa appeared.

Callie and Noelle looked at the mugs of cocoa, licking their lips.

Fairy Princess Snowflurry tapped her wand to her forehead. "Tsk, tsk, tsk. That'll never do." The fairy flicked, swished, and twirled her wand. Glitter fell from the tip and formed four giant marshmallows, which then splashed into the cocoa.

Callie and Noelle blinked. They glanced at each other. Then at the fairy with their mouths wide open in awe.

Swirls of fairy dust trailed from the mugs as the fairy floated them over to the two friends. "Do you still think I'm not to be trusted?"

With the mug at her feet, Callie watched as streams of clover-shaped steam rose into the air. She leaned closer and smelled the cocoa's sugary sweetness. Callie took a sip. "Yummm. It's delicious." She drank it up, warming instantly. "Drink yours," Callie whispered to her friend. She nudged the mug toward Noelle.

"Are you sure it's okay?" Noelle dipped the tip of her beak into the sweet drink.

"Yes," Callie said. "I promise."

"It's delicious." Noelle drank it all down and then hiccuped.

"Now, here's some extra to take on your journey." Fairy Princess Snowflurry waved her wand and a crystal canteen filled with sparkling, pink hollyberry cocoa appeared. "You have had your first wish. I shall grant you two more."

"Only two?" Noelle tweeted. "She really *is* clever and cunning."

"Your friend wished for warmth. I granted it." Fairy Princess Snowflurry fluttered her large butterfly-like wings, laughing gleefully. "Now, quickly, then, tell me your other two wishes."

"Well," Callie said, thinking aloud. "We're on our way to see the king."

"The king? Oh goodness to heavens and Avonlea," Fairy Princess Snowflurry said as she paced about on the path. "Why must you see the king?"

"Because of this," Callie said as she lowered her head to the ground. The straw bag slipped from her mane onto the snow-covered ground.

"What is it?" Fairy Princess Snowflurry bent down and picked up the bag. She opened the small pouch and emptied the contents into her hand. "Oh my!" The fairy princess gasped. "I've heard stories of ice flowers, but…" Fairy Princess Snowflurry paused. "…I didn't think they were true."

Callie looked at Noelle. Her heart leapt in her chest.

"So you've heard of ice flowers?" Noelle tweeted.

"Yes, but that was a long time ago." Snowflurry held the flower between her two fingers. "Where did you find this?"

"Callie made it," Noelle said as she bounced in the air, making her way toward Fairy Princess Snowflurry.

"Remarkable! Can you do it again?" Snowflurry walked toward the two friends, her large wings making a soft, gentle breeze.

Callie shook her head. "I don't think so."

"You've done it once?" The fairy princess placed the flower back in the pouch and tucked them both in Callie's mane.

"Twice," Noelle said, correcting her.

Snowflurry squinted as she tapped her wand in her palm. "What makes you think you can't do it a third time?"

"I don't know how." Callie shook her head. "That's why we're on our way to see the king. We thought he could help us."

"Why don't you just fly there?" the fairy princess asked. "You both have wings and you could be there in no time."

Callie stared at the ground. "I don't know how to do that either."

"Well then," Snowflurry said as she stepped back, fluttering her wings. "Then my wishes have come at a perfect time, haven't they?"

"Yes, they have." Callie nodded without looking up. "Thank you, Fairy Princess Snowflurry."

"But what do we wish for?" Noelle chirped.

"Maybe we should wish for protection." Callie lifted her head just a little and turned to see Noelle nodding in agreement.

The fairy tapped her wand to Callie's head. "I hereby grant thee protection." A glass container appeared at Callie's feet. The fairy picked it up and handed it to Noelle.

"Bubbles?" Noelle tucked the cylinder-shaped container under her wing.

"Just open the bottle and blow on the wand. The rest will take care of itself." Fairy Princess Snowflurry patted the little bird on her head.

"Thank you," Callie said as she lifted her gaze. She smiled at the fairy, feeling very grateful for these wishes.

"You're very welcome, Miss Callie," Snowflurry said as she looked into Callie's big, violet-colored eyes. "Now, you have one final wish."

"There's only one thing else we need," Callie said. "And I think I know exactly what it is."

"We have warmth and safety." Noelle tucked the bottle of bubbles in Callie's mane. "And the warmth is also our food."

"The only thing missing is light," Callie said. "When it grows dark, we'll want to light our path."

"Good thinking," Noelle said in agreement.

"We wish for light." Callie pawed at the ground in excitement.

The fairy waved her wand and a silver lantern appeared. "Your wish is granted."

"But there's no flame," Callie said. "How can it light our path?"

"It's a magical lantern." Snowflurry smiled. "As soon as the sun sets, the lantern will light itself."

"Ohhhh." Noelle flew to the ground and tried to pick up the large lantern with her beak.

The fairy watched as Noelle struggled with the heavy item. She looked at the canteen on the ground and the bottle of bubbles in Callie's mane. "Tsk, tsk, tsk. Oh my, no, that will never do." Fairy Princess Snowflurry waved her wand and a golden rope appeared. "I have a solution." The fairy threaded the rope through the handle of the lantern, the top of the bottle of bubbles, and through the cap of the canteen. Then she tied it all in a bow around Callie's neck. "That's much better."

"It makes a beautiful necklace," Callie said. "Thank you."

"Now, off you go. Hurry, before the storm sets in." Snowflurry nudged Callie with her wand.

"Thank you for the gifts." Callie pawed at the ground.

Noelle twittered in the air before landing on Callie's horn. "They're very much appreciated."

"I have no doubt you'll put them to good use." The fairy lifted into the sky, twirled in the air, and showered glitter on the friends as she disappeared right before their eyes.

"She left as mysteriously as she arrived," Callie said.

Noelle whispered, her voice filled with awe, "Fairy princesses are strange, but beautiful."

"Yes, they are." Callie bowed her head in respect. "Thank you, Fairy Princess Snowflurry. We'll never forget your kindness."

Soon Callie started once again, with Noelle perched atop her horn, on her journey to meet the king. Now equipped with proper tools—special gifts from the fairy—she felt more prepared and a little less scared. Callie's hooves sunk into the snow as she stepped on the path around the winding turn of the mountain.

"Oh, and a word of caution," the fairy's voice called out on the wind.

Callie stopped to listen to Fairy Princess Snowflurry's advice.

"There are slumbering creatures ahead. Best not to wake them."

"We wouldn't dream of it," Callie said with a neigh. With that, the two friends continued on their journey up the mountain to meet King Hollyberry.

As Callie approached a steep incline, the wind snapped at her face. She turned away, her cheeks stinging. When she opened her eyes, she noticed the sun sinking in the horizon. "We will need to hurry," she said. "Or we will have to journey through the dark."

"Don't worry," Noelle said. "We have the light from the fairy. All will be well."

This was true, but Callie didn't want to travel at night. "There are creatures who only come out in the dark. What if they try to harm us?"

"No need to fear." Noelle patted Callie's head. "We have protection from the fairy."

Again, her friend was correct.

"Besides, if you hurry, you might slip on the icy path and we have no gifts of healing."

"You're right," Callie said, thinking about the icy path. "Best to be careful then."

"Just take it one step at a time and we'll be there soon enough." Noelle was a wise friend and Callie felt grateful to have her share this journey with her.

The mountain grew steeper with each step Callie took.

Her legs grew tired.

The sky grew dark.

The friends grew cold.

"Maybe we should rest a bit," Callie said as she shook the fresh snow from her coat. Noelle flew off and landed on a tree branch sticking out of the cliff. She shivered.

Callie felt bad her friend was cold. "You must be tired."

The sun began to set in the distance and the lantern on Callie's neck started to glow. "Look at that!" Callie said as she pointed her hoof at the lantern's light on the snow-covered ground. "It's a rainbow."

"It really is a magical light." Noelle winged her way off the branch down to the ground and inspected the lantern closer. "I'm glad you trusted her."

Callie whinnied. "Me, too." She started along the path. She was grateful for the light. It would help them on their journey. Soon they'd reach the king and have answers! Callie remembered to step carefully despite her excitement. As she rounded a turn, she spied something that stopped her in her tracks.

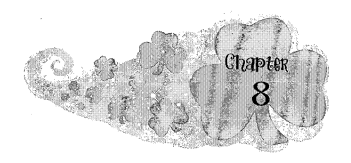

"The path is blocked," Callie said, pointing at a mound of rocks. "Look!"

Noelle darted along the path. She looked up and saw that a portion of the mountain had tumbled down creating an obstacle of rocks. "Looks like an avalanche. There's no way around it."

"Are you sure?" Callie trotted toward her friend.

Noelle nodded. As she glanced at the trail she saw it was worse that she feared. "Don't come any closer," Noelle held her wing out. "Part of the trail has collapsed."

Callie backed up slowly. She didn't want to fall. She certainly wasn't ready to use her wings. All she wanted was an answer about the

ice flower. "Now we'll never get to see Ki
Hollyberry."

Suddenly, the light from her rainbow
lantern began to grow brighter. The beam of
light was so bright, it was as if it were midday.
Callie squinted, and then closed her eyes,
shielding them from the glare. A moment later,
the light began to dim again. As Callie opened
her eyes, she saw a rainbow. The arch stretched
from the path in front of her to a cliff above
them. "Would you look at that! A rainbow
path!"

"I think that might be our chance!" Noelle
perched on Callie's horn.

Callie reared up in excitement. "The fairy
princess was so kind. The rainbow lantern has
given us a way to continue our journey. She
must really want us to reach the king!"

"What's even better, it's a shortcut, too!"
Noelle said.

"A shortcut?" Callie turned to study the
trail they'd been taking. It hadn't been terrible
but even if they could get past the avalanche,
the path was terribly narrow. Plus, it was steep
and littered with debris as it spiraled around

43

the mountain. "You're right! Without the rainbow helping us up to the next level, we'd have to climb that dangerous looking part of the trail." Callie smiled at the colors arched before her, grateful for the shortcut. The arch had a graceful curve but it looked as smooth as glass. "Do you think the rainbow is slippery?"

"It could be." Noelle flew off Callie's horn toward the rainbow arch. She sat on it and slid right off. "It's very slippery. You're going to have to be careful."

"I will. But I may need your help." Callie headed toward the rainbow. When she reached it, she placed her front hoof on it. The rainbow was as slick as ice. "This is going to be tricky but I think I can do it." She backed up a few steps, trying to gain her footing. She took a deep breath, put her head down, and charged straight ahead, running up the rainbow. She made it halfway, but lost her footing and slid all the way back down. "This is harder than it looks," Callie said to Noelle. "It's much too slippery."

"Try again. I'm sure you can do it."

"Alright." Callie backed up and got another

running start. Again, she got halfway up the arch and slid back down. She flapped her wings frantically.

"You can do it, Callie," Noelle cried. "Just try a little harder."

"I can't get enough of a running start. If I could back up further, I'm sure I could do it."

"We'll have to come up with another idea," Noelle said.

Callie thought about a way to use the rainbow to her advantage. Climbing wouldn't work because the surface was too slippery. She couldn't just walk up it. There wasn't enough room to get a running start. There had to be another way. Surely, the fairy princess wouldn't grant them a bad wish. There had to be some secret magic to this rainbow. Callie just needed to figure out what it was. She so desperately wanted to see King Hollyberry and get answers.

"What if we use the rope necklace that Fairy Princess Snowflurry gave you?" Noelle flew up over the rainbow to the cliff. She pointed at a tree. "We could tie it around the branch. Then you can grab onto the rope with your teeth and pull yourself up the rest of the way."

"That's a great idea." Callie nodded. Then she started to think about the lantern, the canteen, and the bubbles all threaded onto the necklace. "But if we use the rope, then who will carry the gifts? The lantern is too heavy for you and it'll slide off my back."

"Hmmm…." Noelle flew back down and tapped her feathered wing to her head. "That's a good point. We'll just have to think of something else."

"Let me think," Callie said as she began to walk on the narrow mountain path toward the boulder. It was getting colder and she shivered. She was getting tired and she yawned.

"Maybe we should drink some of the cocoa. It might give us some energy." Noelle removed the canteen from Callie's necklace and flew back toward the rainbow for some light. She unscrewed the cap. Just as she was about to pour some of the magical cocoa into the canteen's cap, it slipped from her feathered wings and fell to the ground. The pink drink leaked onto the snowy path. "Oh no!"

"What happened?" Callie trotted toward her friend. She slipped on the ice and landed right into the puddle of pink cocoa.

"I thought a drink might help, but I've spilled it everywhere." Noelle hung her head. "Now we have no warmth *or* food."

Callie licked the sugary drink from her fur. "It's very sticky." She lifted her hoof. Great big wads of it clung to her hooves. "It's very gummy." When she took a step, the pink drink stayed glued to her like a glob of gumberries. "So very sticky and gummy." Callie lit up with excitement as she glanced at the rainbow. "I think I have an idea."

"*A*n idea! That's wonderful, Callie!" Noelle winged her way toward her friend. "What is it?"

"The cocoa is so sticky it's like gumberries." Callie lifted her front hoof. She showed her friend the sticky pink glue. "The sticky cocoa might help my hooves attach to the slick surface of the rainbow. I think I might be able to walk right over it!"

"Let's try it!" Noelle flittered about in excitement.

Callie stepped in the cocoa, making sure to coat all four of her hooves. "I'm ready." As soon as Noelle was safely perched on Callie's head, they started toward the rainbow. Callie placed one hoof on the slippery surface. It stuck there tight and fast, just as she'd hoped.

"I think it's going to work," she said to her friend. She stepped another hoof onto the rainbow, then another, until all four hooves were safely secured on the arch.

"Can you go further?" Noelle asked.

"I think so." Callie tried to lift her front hoof, but it was really stuck! "This will be harder than I thought."

"Keep trying," Noelle said.

Callie inched her way forward, up the rainbow. She peeled each hoof free, then stuck it down again, step by step until she was just inches from the top. When she saw the cliff, she was as happy as a narwhal in the Dragon Sea. "Almost there!" She climbed over the edge and landed safely.

Noelle kissed the top of Callie's head. "You did it!"

"Yes, I did," Callie said, feeling very, very proud of herself. She had done something very hard. If she could climb a rainbow, there was no telling what else she might be able to do. Including, maybe, fly.

In her excitement, she reared up on her hind legs. A wind whipped around the mountain and Callie braced herself against it. Her wings flapped. Her heart beat wildly. When her front hooves landed, sparks shot out.

"Look! Another ice flower!" Callie cried, seeing what she'd made.

"So it is!" Noelle chirped. "I'll get it so we can bring it to the king."

"Good idea," Callie said. "But we must hurry. It's getting darker and I'm growing tired."

Noelle shivered. "I need to get warm." She carried the ice flower from the ground and placed it inside the woven bag on top of Callie's head.

The lantern glowed its rainbow light and lit their path. "Now we can be on our way," Callie said, walking ahead. With each step she took, the sticky hollyberry cocoa washed off in the snow.

The two continued on their journey on the steep and snowy mountain path. As the night grew darker, the air grew colder. Callie shivered in the wind. "I think we should stop and rest a bit," she said. "It's much too cold and we are out of cocoa. We will need to find another way to stay warm. If we wait until morning, we'll have sunlight to light our path and warm our bodies."

"I agree," Noelle said with a shiver. "There's a cave up ahead." She pointed with a feathered wing toward a dark spot in the side of the mountain.

"It looks like a perfect place to rest," Callie said. "We'll be protected from the cold and the wind."

Noelle tweeted the song of Wintersend as she entered the cave. Callie followed close behind, the rainbow lantern casting colorful hues of pinks, yellows, greens, blues, and purples. The colors bounced about, creating a beautiful glow.

Callie spied a pile of evergreen branches. "This looks like a cozy spot to snuggle in for a rest." She settled down into the nest. The branches were warm and snug beneath her fur. She began to doze off into a nice slumber. Moments later, she awakened to a tickling in her nose. Callie began to sneeze.

One sneeze.

A second sneeze.

A third sneeze.

"Shhhhh," Noelle said. "Did you hear that?"

A low growl echoed in the cave. "What's that sound?" Callie asked.

"I'm not sure," Noelle replied. She hovered in the air, listening. "Let me go check. I will be right back."

Callie looked up from her bed of evergreens. "Be careful, Noelle."

Noelle nodded and then flew off into the darkness. She returned a moment later. "Callie, we must leave. Quickly, friend!"

"What's wrong? What is it?" Callie sprung to her feet, stirring the bedding.

"It's a snow monster."

"A snow monster?" Callie's eyes grew large. "Oh no! This is exactly what the fairy warned us about."

"I think you're right," said Noelle. "He's snoring in his sleep but he's tossing and turning, too. He looks like he will wake up any moment. We can escape as long as we sneak out quickly. But we must be quiet."

"What are we waiting for?" Callie whispered. As she said this, her hooves rustled the evergreens. Callie felt her nose twitch. "Oh no! I think I'm allergic."

"Allergic?" Noelle cried. "To what?"

"The junipers," Callie said. "They must have been in my bed." She wrinkled her nose to stop the sneeze, which threatened to wake the monster.

Noelle put her feathered wing to the tip of Callie's nose. "Hold it in or else you'll wake him. Then he'll be really angry."

"I...I...I..." Callie stammered as she tried to contain the sneeze. Her eyes watered. "I... I...I..." Callie's nose tickled and twitched. "I... I...I... ACHOO!" Callie sneezed so loud, it echoed inside the cave. It shook the walls.

A great and terrible roar echoed throughout the cavern.

"We must go!" Noelle cried.

Callie's fear was true. "It's too late."

The lantern's soft light illuminated the figure of a large, white snow bear.

Chapter 10

*I*t wasn't exactly a monster like Noelle had claimed. Snow bears were massive creatures with large claws and shaggy white fur. Except they were make believe. They weren't real. At least that's what Callie had always thought.

The giant snow bear lumbered toward them. He roared again showing his large, sharp teeth. His giant, fur-covered body smelled like rotten clovers. Callie stumbled backward. The snow bear towered over her and Callie trembled in fear.

"They are real," Callie said.

"We have to escape." Noelle pointed to the opening where they'd first entered the cave for a rest.

"We can't go out that way. He'll follow us!"

"Then what should we do?"

Callie had another clever idea. "We need to trick him."

"How do we do that?" Noelle flapped her wings as fast as a hummingbird.

"If you buzz around his head, it might distract him. Lead him down that way." Callie pointed at a small, narrow tunnel. "He'll have to squeeze in and might get stuck. Then you can fly out to safety."

"I can do that," Noelle said. She flew up and around the bear's head. The snow bear growled. He lifted both hands in the air and swatted at Noelle. She was swift and nimble and darted out of the way. "Follow me, Mr. Snow Bear." She flew toward the narrow tunnel and the bear trailed behind, batting his hands in the air as if he were trying to squish a mosquito.

"It's working!" Callie said. "Keep going!"

"We'll be safe soon!" Noelle chirped and twittered off into the distance. The bear's large feet slapped against the cavern's stone floor.

Callie crept toward them, the lantern shining a rainbow path into the tunnel. Callie watched as Noelle darted into the darkness and the creature followed. A few moments passed and there was no sign of Noelle. Callie began to fear for her friend. She hadn't thought that Noelle might get stuck in there with the bear. What had she done? If she'd brought harm to her dear friend, Callie would never forgive herself.

"Noelle!" Callie cried. "Are you alright?"

A small tweet came sweetly through the cave.

"Noelle! Follow my voice. Follow the rainbow!"

Tweet, tweet.

Callie reared up, shining the lantern's light higher. She could see white fur sticking out of the tunnel. The bear was wedged in tight. There was no way for her friend to escape. "Noelle, I'm sorry!" A tear dripped from her eye.

Tweet, tweet. The bird's call grew louder. Tweet, tweet. Suddenly, Noelle darted between the bear's legs and flew out of the tunnel.

"You're okay!" In her excitement, Callie trotted in a circle. When she looked again at the tunnel, she saw the bear wiggling his way out. "Hurry, Noelle! Hurry!"

Noelle flew toward Callie, but the bear escaped. He clomped toward them, his monstrously large feet making a bass drum-like sound as they slapped against the floor. The bear swatted at the air and Noelle bounced on the wind he created. He was closing in on her tail feathers.

"Use the bubbles from the fairy," Noelle chirped.

Remembering their special gift, Callie dipped her head down, letting the necklace slip from her neck. The bottle tumbled to the ground. Noelle quickly scooped it up with her feathers. She opened the cap and blew a bubble.

It was the largest bubble Callie had ever seen. It quickly surrounded the two friends, embracing them into its safety. The bubble lifted into the air. The bear swatted at the bubble and it bounced around in the air.

"Ahhhh!" Callie screamed. "He's going to get us!"

They friends started to float away, out of

the cave and away from the snow bear. "We're going to be okay." Noelle's tweet sounded tired.

"Are you sure?" Callie looked down at the cave and saw they were out of reach of the bear. Too far, in fact. The bubble floated higher and higher. Callie started to tremble. They were too high! "We must get down!" Callie cried.

"We're floating to safety," Noelle sang.

"This doesn't feel safe." No, it wasn't safe at all. *This is what flying must feel like*, she thought. *It's much too scary. I knew I'd never be able to fly.* "I'm scared," Callie said as she reared up on her hind legs, flapping her wings.

"Calm down," Noelle said. "You might pop the bubble and then we'll fall. Just let it carry you. We'll be safe. Fairy Princess Snowflurry promised us."

"Are you sure?" Callie wasn't sure, but she really wanted to believe her friend.

Noelle perched on Callie's horn. "Yes."

Callie brought her wings back in close to her body and lowered her hooves. She still felt scared as they floated higher and higher. She took a deep breath as the bubble carried them up the mountainside.

As Callie looked down, she saw the snow bear standing on the cliff outside the cave. He had his hands in the air as if he was reaching for them. Thankfully, they were safe, just as the fairy had assured them.

Callie soon calmed even though she had always been so afraid of flying. "Is this what flying feels like?" Callie asked her friend. The bubble bounced about on the breeze. Callie felt like a seasick sea lizard. "If it is, then I don't think I will ever like flying."

"It's similar, but not the same." Noelle tweeted a happy little tweet. "The bubble is controlled by the wind. When you fly, *you* control your wings and steer wherever you like."

Callie sighed with relief. If she could control her wings, then she could make all the choices about her flight. Maybe it wouldn't be as bad as she thought. In fact, she smiled, thinking it might even be fun.

The bubble floated higher. As it lifted into the air and up the mountainside, the rainbow lantern began to dim. In the distance, the sun began to rise. The higher the bubble carried them, the brighter it became.

"It's morning," Callie said, distracted by the sun's beautiful rays. She didn't see the side of the mountain. She didn't see anything except the golden sunlight.

"That's it!" Noelle said as she pointed down at an icy throne carved into an opening at the top of the mountain. "There's King Hollyberry's castle. And there he is, sitting on his throne!"

Chapter 11

The bubble didn't stop. It floated higher and higher. Soon the king became a tiny speck.

"Oh no!" Callie cried. "We're too high. We need to get back down to the mountain."

"You'll need to use your wings," Noelle said. "Just a few small breezes will bring us back."

"Are you sure it will work?" Callie asked. "What if it takes us higher?"

"It won't," Noelle assured. "I'd do it myself, but my wings aren't as big as yours."

"That's true," Callie said. "Just three little flaps?"

"Yes," Noelle said. "That should do it."

Callie carefully brought her wings forward. If she stretched them out too wide, the bubble might burst. Then they'd fall to the ground. Well, Noelle would use her wings to fly, but Callie wasn't sure if she would be able to control her own in an emergency. She wasn't going to take that chance either.

As she drew her wings back, the bubble moved forward and went closer to the king.

"It's working, Callie! Good job!" Noelle tweeted with excitement as she bounced around inside the bubble.

"It really is!" Callie was so happy. She had controlled her wings! She flapped them two more times, bringing the bubble down, down, down. In that moment, she wasn't scared. "I did it!" Callie whinnied with joy.

The bubble drifted closer and closer until they nearly reached the king. He sat on his throne, holding an icicle staff in his hand. King Hollyberry had a long white beard and wore a crown of the pink berries on his head. White fur trimmed the edges of his pale, blue cloak. The fabric fluttered softly in the breeze as Callie's bubble approached.

King Hollyberry stood and banged his staff on the ground. Callie reared up, frantically.

"Don't be afraid," Noelle said.

"But he looks angry," Callie said as she watched the king pound the staff again.

"I certainly hope not. Maybe he's excited to have visitors." Noelle patted her friend's head. "We're almost there. If you're careful, we'll float right up to the king's throne."

Callie breathed deeply. "All right. If you say so." She lifted her wings again. "Just one last flap should do it." She brought her wings forward. Just as she expected, the bubble carried them straight to the king. They landed at his feet as he stood near his throne.

"We've come to speak with you," Callie shouted through the bubble.

"We have gifts," Noelle said.

"Not yet," Callie whispered to her. "Maybe we should show him the flowers later."

"But that's the reason we've come to see him." Noelle scratched her feathered wing to her head.

"Is it all right if we have a moment with you?" Callie asked the king.

King Hollyberry said something in return, but Callie could only see his lips move.

"I can't hear you," Callie called through the bubble. Just as she was about to lean forward, the king lifted his staff into the air. He held it over the bubble, his eyes narrowing, and Callie cowered in fear. The king's staff glistened in the cold winter air, the sun reflecting off its surface, as he struck it on the bubble.

Chapter 12

"*W*atch out!" Noelle said as she ducked behind Callie's ear.

King Hollyberry's staff hit the bubble with so much force, the glass shattered everywhere, raining down like glitter.

Callie bowed in front of the king. "We've come to see you," she said, her legs shaking and her heart thudding.

"Why have you come to see me?" The king's voice boomed like thunder, each word louder than the first.

Callie looked up, her knees still firmly planted on the ground. "We've found something magical."

"Magical?" King Hollyberry's voice softened as he stroked his long, white beard.

"Yes, and we've brought gifts," Noelle said.

The king held out his hand. "What kind of gifts?"

"Ice flowers." Callie stood on shaky legs.

Noelle lifted the woven straw bag from Callie's mane. She dropped the bag into the king's palm. "Magical ice flowers."

The king opened the bag and shook the two ice flowers into his hand. "Well, isn't that remarkable? I have never seen anything like it! But..." King Hollyberry paused as he studied the flowers. "There have been tales."

"Tales? About the ice flowers?" Callie looked at Noelle in surprise.

"Oh, yes," the king said. "Long ago."

Callie nudged Noelle. "Fairy Princess Snowflurry said there were stories, too."

"You saw Snowflurry?" King Hollyberry gasped in surprise.

"Yes," said Callie. "She granted us three wishes. If not for her, we'd never have made it here. That bubble was of her making."

"This is all very interesting." King Hollyberry stroked his beard as he paced back and forth. "No one has ever seen Fairy Princess Snowflurry. The fable said she would only appear for one certain unicorn." He stopped in front of his throne and leaned on his staff.

"One unicorn? Callie gasped.

King Hollyberry straightened. "Yes. Only one."

Callie couldn't believe what she was hearing. Why would Fairy Princess Snowflurry choose to show herself only to one unicorn? *Why was that unicorn me?* she thought. "Is it also true that winter is ending in the Kingdom of Wintersend?" Callie approached the king, keeping her wings close to her side. "My friend Maribel warned me before she came to visit you."

"This is true." The king sat in his throne and folded his hands together. "Your friend left not long ago." King Hollyberry furrowed his brow. "Maribel was right. Winter is ending in Wintersend."

Noelle chirped and flew toward the king. "What can be done?"

The king removed his pink hollyberry crown and scratched his head. "There is only one who can save winter."

"Someone can save winter? Who is it?"

Callie neighed as she pawed a hoof at the ground.

The king placed his crown back on his head. "A very special pegacorn."

Callie gasped. "A pegacorn?"

"Yes, but this pegacorn's power is strong. They would be so powerful, they could bring winter to all of the other kingdoms in the Isle of Avonlea and change the island forever."

"Winter in the other kingdoms?" Callie whinnied. The kingdoms never shared their seasons. That would be dangerous! There was a delicate balance on the Isle of Avonlea, and if the seasons were to change, there would be no more colorful clover, pink hollyberries, sparkle fruit, or purple pumpkins for the unicorns and pegacorns to eat.

"Yes, that's why it's important to know where these two ice flowers came from," the king said as he banged his staff on the ground.

Callie flinched and backed away. She didn't want the king to know that she had anything to do with these flowers. It would be a terrible thing to harm the other kingdoms.

"Did you see the pegacorn who created them?" the king asked.

"Callie did," Noelle said.

"You saw the pegacorn?" The king's voice boomed as it had once before.

Callie shook her head. She hadn't seen the pegacorn. She *was* the pegacorn!

"No." Noelle tweeted and chirped, flying about excitedly. "Callie *made* them."

The king lifted his staff into the air and brought it down sharply. It clanged against the ground in a mighty, powerful sound. "Did you really make these?" The king's voice thundered, echoing off the mountaintops.

Callie felt tears forming in her eyes. The king was angry! Now she'd never be willing to fly. She might make a mistake with her powers. *It would be terrible if I harmed the other pegacorns, in Wintersend,* she thought. *It would be awful if I hurt the unicorns in Summerstart, Springsmorn, and Autumnseve. I could ruin all of Avonlea!* Callie felt awful. *If I can't control how I make the flowers, would I even be able to control the weather?* she wondered.

"Tell me," the king roared. "Did you make these?"

Callie shivered in fear. "Yes. I made them." She hung her head.

"Prove it," King Hollyberry banged his staff against the snowy ground. "Make them for me."

"I can't." Callie shook her head. She didn't know how she made them. She only knew that they appeared. She was certain she couldn't make them on command.

King Hollyberry furrowed his brow. "But you just told me you made them."

"Yes, but I don't know *how* I did."

"I don't believe you." The king stepped closer. He looked in Callie's eyes. "Hmmm....Violet eyes. I see the truth is in there." He stepped away. The king cast his gaze at Noelle. "What do you know about it?"

"I saw her make them." Noelle flew to Callie's head. "It's okay, friend," she whispered in Callie's ear. "Don't be afraid." Then Noelle directed her words toward the king. "But she speaks the truth. It was a surprise to her every time they appeared."

"What was she doing when they

appeared?" The king studied the glittering ice flowers again, bringing them up to eye level.

"I was trying *not* to fly," Callie said in shame.

The king's hand trembled. The flowers slipped from his fingers, but he caught them before they shattered to the ground. "What do you mean you were trying not to fly?"

"I've been afraid to take flight. So whenever a breeze comes, I fight it off. When my hooves land, sparks fly, and the flower appears."

"Well, well, well." King Hollyberry turned away. He walked to his throne and placed the ice flowers safely there. When he finished, he turned around sharply. "We will just have to put this to the test."

"A test?" Callie asked. "What kind of test?"

The king held up his staff. He twirled it around and around above his head. A giant gust of wind sent Noelle and Callie sailing through the air.

"*H*elp," Noelle cried as she flapped her little birdie wings. "It's too strong, Callie."

Callie fought against the wind, bringing her hooves back to the ground. She slipped on the ice, but quickly steadied herself, feeling a sudden inner strength against the king's impossible wind. She turned her head, shielding her eyes from the ice crystals that burned her face. "I'm coming, Noelle."

The king watched as Callie stood her ground. "I see my wind isn't quite strong enough!" He lifted his staff into the air. "I'll take care of that." The wind picked up speed. It twirled and twirled in a giant tornado. It blew at Callie in a blast of bitter cold, biting at her face.

"Hold on, my friend," Callie called as Noelle bounced about in the air. "I'll help you." Callie dug her hooves into the ground, keeping her head down as she tried to save her friend.

"That'll never do," the king said as he held his staff high in the air. "You'll never fight this one." He shot a gust of wind so powerful, that it sent Callie sailing over the cliff.

Callie pawed at the mountain's edge. "Help," she cried. "I can't hold on."

"But you don't have to," King Hollyberry said. He banged his staff on the ground again and the wind stopped. "There is another way."

Noelle tumbled to the ground near the edge of the cliff. Her tired wings went limp. "You need to fly, Callie."

Of course! Flight was the only way she could help herself.

Noelle perked her head up. "Stretch out your wings, Callie. Just like you did in the bubble." She showed Callie by trying to lift her own wing into the air, but she was so tired and weak that only a single feather raised off the ground.

Callie opened her wings but her hooves began to slip. "Help," she cried, but her wings began to flap, almost as if they knew what to do.

Seeing her friend succeed, Noelle lifted her head and smiled. "That's right. You've nearly got it." She felt energy return and flittered toward Callie. "You can do it."

Callie flapped her wings again. She began to rise in the air. Her wings carried her higher and higher until she no longer needed to hold onto the side of the cliff.

"Well, well, well," King Hollyberry sang. "Would you look at that?" He laughed in delight. "You *can* fly."

"I can?" Callie flapped her wings. "I mean...yes, I can!" She glanced down and saw that she was very high. Everything in the Kingdom of Wintersend looked like tiny specs. She saw the Glitter Palace in the center of Avonlea, but even it was no larger than a hollyberry. Callie felt sick. She was too high! Her wings trembled. The wind threw her about and her wings faltered. Callie began to fall.

*D*own. Down. Down.

Callie fell lower, lower, and lower. "C'mon wings," she cried. "Don't fail me now." She flapped them hard against the wind, ignoring the tremble of fear that made her whole body feel weak. "I can do this." She squeezed her eyes shut and forced her wings to work. She felt the air beneath them, tickling and working with her. Callie opened her eyes and saw that she was back where she started! She rolled onto the cliff and landed at the king's feet.

"Very good, very good!" King Hollyberry clapped his hands as he laughed. "Now try again."

Callie nodded. She climbed to her feet. A

gust of wind burst toward her and she steadied herself. Then she reared up and came down hard. When she landed, an ice flower appeared.

King Hollyberry looked at her in amazement. "Why, you really *do* make the ice flowers."

"I told you," Noelle said.

Callie nodded. "Yes, your majesty."

"Then you mustn't be afraid to fly." The king waved his wand.

Callie reared up. Her front hooves lifted off the ground. She flapped her wings. Then her rear hooves lifted off the ground, too. Callie glanced down at the ground. When she saw that she was floating in the air, she flapped her beautiful white wings again. She lifted higher and higher. For the first time ever, Callie wasn't scared. She had control of her wings. They didn't control her.

Callie whinnied as she stretched her majestic wings as wide as they could go. She soared through the sky.

"I'm flying," she exclaimed. "I'm really flying!" Her wings were strong and powerful. She flew straight at the king. Just as she was about to dive into him, the king ducked, and Callie quickly steered left. King Hollyberry laughed in delight. Callie climbed higher in the sky, soaring above the mountaintops and through the clouds.

"Look! She's flying," Noelle said to the king. "Fly, Callie! Fly!" She whistled and tweeted with joy.

"So she is." King Hollyberry banged his staff on the ground and watched Callie's magical flight. "I knew you had it in you," he shouted to her.

Callie's heart swelled with joy as she glided through the sky, feeling the magic of her powerful wings.

Her hooves tingled.

They twitched.

They tickled.

Glittery sparkles shot out, creating a trail of glittering snow. The beautiful snowstorm rained down on the Kingdom of Wintersend, coating it in a blanket of white.

"I made snow!" Callie cried with joy. "I made SNOW!" she shouted down to her friend, Noelle, who was still chirping on the cliff below.

"There it is." The king folded his arms with a smile. "The snow that saved Wintersend."

"She has magic," Noelle tweeted.

Callie rose higher in the sky, stirring a breeze so strong, the snow drifted from the mountaintops, dusting the crops in the Kingdom of Springsmorn. She was very powerful. She'd have to be careful or her magic could harm the balance in Avonlea. "Hello, friends!" she called to the unicorns in Springsmorn. She watched as all the unicorns gathered and knelt in awe.

Callie flew south to Summerstart and shook the trees with her breeze. The trail of snow from her hooves turned to rain and the unicorns danced with delight. As Callie flew off, a rainbow formed in the sky stretching from one end of Summerstart to the other.

When Callie reached Autmnseve, the dragon fire had gone out and the unicorns cheered her name.

Callie returned to Wintersend. The king and Noelle waved at her. Callie waved back. She had saved winter! This flight – and Callie's magic – was a gift. Callie knew it and so did all the other unicorns and pegacorns on the Isle of Avonlea. With powerful gifts comes an important responsibility. Callie would have to respect her magic. Someday, she thought, she might need to help her kingdom again. Callie would be prepared. She wouldn't be afraid.

She flew one final loop and landed on top of Mount Wintersend.

King Hollyberry cheered. "You're a powerful one!" He crowned Callie with a wreath of berries. He gently tapped her shoulders with his staff. "I officially pronounce thee Callie, Princess Pegacorn of Winter. The very pegacorn that was foretold to save the Kingdom of Wintersend."

"It is my honor." Callie reared up on her hind legs and flapped her wings with a loud whinny.

"You have magic," Noelle said with a chirp.

"It is a special gift." Callie was glad she

When mischievous pixies threaten a special friendship, Maeve must find the magic within herself to save them both.

Turn the page for a peek at *Maeve's New Friend*, book two in the Unicorn Tales series!

*T*here was magic in the Kingdom of Springsmorn and Maeve loved living there. Rainbow River glistened with beautiful colors as it flowed toward the south end of Avonlea. Magical fish splashed about in Blossom Lagoon asking for playmates. The Sparkle Fruit Garden was always ripe with juicy, green fruit. Springsmorn offered a unicorn everything they could ever want. Despite all of this Maeve was missing one thing; her magic.

Maeve enjoyed dancing in the rainstorms that helped feed the gardens. She lazed around on the sunny days that made the sparkle fruit grow. She pranced in the warm breezes that tickled her fur. Her favorite activity was going to the flower field surrounding the lagoon.

There she could watch the damselflies dart about as they touched earth and sky. Without her magic, though, the enchantment of Springsmorn began to fade.

Maeve shook her powdery blue mane in the spring breeze. It was a beautiful day for a stroll and she wanted nothing more than to sun her dappled gray coat in the warmth of the meadow. Perhaps her magic was in the special place she loved so much. Maybe she'd find it there.

"I'm so lucky to live in the Kingdom of Springsmorn," she thought aloud. "It would be even better if I could find my magic." Her stomach growled. "But I must first have a snack." Maeve plucked a glittering green sparkle fruit from the tree. She crunched into it, the sweetness twirling on her tongue. She ate it in three quick bites.

Maeve's friend Shannon pranced up to her. "What are you doing?" Shannon asked as she shook her blonde mane. Her golden coat shimmered in the sunshine. The two were good friends and Maeve always appreciated Shannon's wisdom. Shannon had more knowledge than any unicorn or pegacorn in all of Avonlea. Maeve had an idea. Maybe Shannon knew where to find Maeve's magic.

"I was just finishing a snack," Maeve said as she watched Shannon pick an apple from the tree. Maeve stared in awe as a new apple immediately began to grow in its place. "I thought you might know where my magic was. I've been longing to find it. Do you think you can help me?"

"I couldn't help you with that," Shannon said as she took a bite of the fruit. Her mouth was full but she continued to speak anyway. "Pw-ix-ips…" Pieces of the fruit fell to the ground.

"What was that?" Maeve asked as she watched her friend eat another piece of sparkle fruit.

This time Shannon finished the fruit before speaking. "The pixies," she said, suddenly lowering her voice. "The pixies are up to their pranks again. I have to settle it before it gets out of hand."

"Pranks?" Maeve's tail twitched. Her horn felt tingly. "Why must they do such things?"

Shannon shook her head. "It's amusement for them. They don't realize the harm that comes from their tricks."

"What can we do?" Maeve studied Shannon's face hoping to gain her wisdom.

"I'm headed to Star Hollow to speak with Willow."

Maeve squinted in confusion. "The tree?"

"Of course! Willow has insight. She might be able to talk to the pixies on behalf of the unicorns."

"That's brilliant, Shannon." Maeve whinnied, shaking her head in excitement. The thought of going to Star Hollow, which was right next to Pixie Place, terrified Maeve. She didn't want the pixies to play a prank on her. She also didn't want to look like she was afraid, either. "Would you like company? I could come with you."

"This is best handled alone." Shannon neighed. "I'm sure you have lots to do today. You need to find your magic, after all. That'll keep you quite busy. I'll tell you all about it when I return."

Maeve sighed with relief. "Have a safe journey, my friend." She was disappointed, though, too. Finding her magic was going to be a difficult task and she thought it might be easier in the company of friends. Now she'd have to search by herself.

"See you soon!" Shannon bowed. "And good luck finding your magic!" She then galloped off toward Star Hollow.

Maeve watched her friend disappear into the woods. She noticed the sunlight filtering through the leafy treetops, casting little gems of gold on the ground. She glanced up at the sky admiring the large, fluffy clouds. In their shapes, she spied a mermaid and a narwhal. *Do I also see a pixie?* she wondered. She blinked. No, her eyes were just playing tricks on her.

A NOTE FROM THE AUTHOR

It is such an honor to share my Unicorn Tales stories with you! Thank you so much for reading them!

When I was a young girl, I was in love with unicorns. After a trip to Scotland in the fall of 2017, where the unicorn is the national animal, my childhood love was rekindled. I couldn't wait to write a series of unicorn stories that would appeal to my childhood self! I hoped they would appeal to young readers who love unicorns as much as I do.

As a writer, I wanted to go a step further and honor Scotland, Ireland, and some of the other countries that inspired the series. This required a study of Celtic legends, myths, and folktales. You'll notice a nod to these Celtic roots in some of the unicorn's names, the series symbol (Celtic knot), the chapter heading (shamrock) and some of the stories themselves! It was so much fun for me to conduct research and bring these unicorns to life! I hope this series has inspired you, too!

There's nothing better than matching readers with great books. If you enjoyed this book, please leave an honest review. Reviews help authors reach more readers.

Thank you for your support!

— Amie Borst

ABOUT THE AUTHOR

Amie Borst believes in unicorns, loves glitter, and keeps a stash of chocolate hidden away from her chocolate-stealing family. She is the author of several books for children including the Scarily Ever Laughter series (Cinderskella, Little Dead Riding Hood, Snow Fright), the Unicorn Tales series, and the Doomy Prepper series (coming September 2019). Visit her website for more information. While you're there, be sure to sign up for her newsletter so you can receive updates on new books, sales, and promotions.

Website: www.amieborst.com

facebook.com/AmieBorstAuthor

instagram.com/AmieBorst

ABOUT THE ILLUSTRATOR

Roch Hercka is an artist, illustrator, painter, and book lover. This is his second children's book series, having previously illustrated the Scarily Ever Laughter series. Roch enjoys painting, reading comic books, playing board games, and watching movies. He lives in Torun, Poland with his family and a cat. Visit his websites to see more of his beautiful creations!

Illustrations: www.hercka.carbonmade.com

Paintings: www.roch.carbonmade.com

facebook.com/RochHerckaArt

instagram.com/Rochart_85